Willa Bean
to the
Rescue!

Little Wings
5

Willa Bean
to the Rescue!

by Cecilia Galante
illustrated by Kristi Valiant

A STEPPING STONE BOOK™

Random House New York

To Emmy and Macy,
the coolest girls in Chicago! —C.G.

For you if you've been bullied or are a bully—
may you find confidence and help. (Psalm 27)
—K.V.

Text copyright © 2013 by Cecilia Galante
Cover art and interior illustrations copyright © 2013 by Kristi Valiant

Visit us on the Web!
SteppingStonesBooks.com
randomhouse.com/kids

Educators and librarians, for a variety of teaching tools, visit us at
RHTeachersLibrarians.com

Library of Congress Cataloging-in-Publication Data
Galante, Cecilia.
Willa Bean to the rescue! / by Cecilia Galante ; illustrated by Kristi Valiant.
— First edition.
p. cm. — (Little wings ; 5)
"A Stepping Stone book."
Summary: "Willa Bean travels down to Earth for the first time with her father on a cupid assignment, where she finds a boy who has been bullied and needs her help."
— Provided by publisher.
ISBN 978-0-449-81003-3 (pbk.) — ISBN 978-0-449-81004-0 (lib. bdg.) —
ISBN 978-0-449-81005-7 (ebook)
1. Cupid (Roman deity)—Juvenile fiction. [1. Cupid (Roman deity)—Fiction.
2. Fathers and daughters—Fiction. 3. Bullying—Fiction.] I. Valiant, Kristi, illustrator.
II. Title.
PZ7.G12965Wg 2013 [Fic]—dc23 2012033886

Printed in the United States of America

10 9 8 7 6 5 4 3 2 1

Contents

Willa Bean's World

Willa Bean Skylight is a cupid. Cupids live in a faraway place called Nimbus, which sits just alongside the North Star, in a tiny pocket of the Milky Way. Nimbus is made up of three white stars and nine clouds, all connected by feather bridges. It has a Cupid Academy, where cupids go to school, a garden cloud, where they grow and store their food, and lots and lots of playgrounds.

Willa Bean lives on Cloud Four with her mother and father, her big sister, Ariel, and her baby brother, Louie. Cloud Four is soft and green. The air around it smells like rain and pineapples. Best of all, Willa Bean's best friend, Harper, also lives on Cloud Four, just a few cloudbumps away.

When cupids are ready, they are given special Earth tasks. That means they have to fly down to Earth to help someone who is having a hard time. Big cupids, like Willa Bean's parents, help Earth grown-ups with things like falling in love. Little cupids, like Willa Bean, help Earth kids if they feel mad, sad, or just plain stuck. Working with Earth people is the most important job a cupid has. It can be hard work, too, but there's nothing that Willa Bean would rather do.

Are you ready for a peek into Willa Bean's world? It's just a few cloudbumps away, so let's go!

Chapter 1

A Moody Moonday

Willa Bean slumped in her chair at the breakfast table and fiddled with one of her curls. It was Moonday, but she was still dressed in her yellow pajamas with pink polka dots. She had not brushed her teeth or untangled her hair. She had not even made her bed, which she had to do every morning before school.

Willa Bean had a good reason for not doing any of these things. The Cupid Academy was closed. And not just for today, but for two whole days. There was a leak in the roof, and until it was fixed, there would be no school. Usually, this would have had Willa Bean flying around the house, squealing for joy.

But not today.

Today she was annoyed. And irritated. And maybe even a little bit angry, too.

"How can you possibly be so glum, Willa Bean?" Mama asked, spooning oatmeal into Baby Louie's mouth. "You have two whole days off from school!"

"Skoo!" Baby Louie shouted.

Willa Bean frowned at her baby brother. "You hush," she said.

"Hush!" Baby Louie shouted.

Willa Bean rolled her eyes. She loved her baby brother, but he could be very annoying at times. Actually, he could be very annoying most of the time.

"What's wrong, sweetheart?" Mama asked gently.

Willa Bean slumped lower in her chair. "Harper's gone," she grumbled. "Her mom and dad took her last night to visit her grandma on Saturn. Even though we already made plans for today and everything!"

"Ah." Mama nodded. "Well, grandmas are important. They need to be visited often, especially if they live far away. How do you think your grandma Vega would feel if we never went to visit her?"

"Hmph," said Willa Bean.

"What kind of plans did you have with Harper?" asked Mama.

"First, we were going to fly to Cloud Five and dig up our treasure chest," Willa Bean said. "I found six new pieces of treasure, and Harper found three. And then we were going to take everything out of the treasure chest and count it. And then we were going to clean every single piece until it was super-shiny and put them all back inside. After that, we were going to go back to Harper's house and make Snoogy Bars and play with Snooze and Octavius."

Snooze was Willa Bean's flying friend. He was a pygmy owl from France. He had brown feathers and big yellow eyes. Octavius was Harper's flying friend. He was a bat. His favorite thing to do was sleep.

"Well, I'm sorry everything got canceled," Mama said. "What about Snooze? I'm sure he'd love to do something with you today."

"Mama." Willa Bean looked at her mother carefully. "Snooze is an *owl*. He sleeps all day. Sometimes he gets up in the afternoon, but only if we have special plans."

"It sounds as if you're just going to have to fly solo for a little while," Mama answered.

"What's *solo*?" Willa Bean asked.

"By yourself." Mama wiped a blob of oatmeal off the corner of Baby Louie's mouth. "But there's nothing wrong with that. Is there any reason why you can't go to Cloud Five and dig up the treasure chest yourself?"

"Yes," Willa Bean said quickly. "Because Harper and I *never* go to the treasure chest by ourselves. It's against the rules."

"Oh," Mama said. "All right. I guess the treasure part of things will have to wait. What about the Snoogy Bars? You can make them here if you want."

"No, I can't," said Willa Bean.

"Why not?" asked Mama.

"Because no one ever makes Snoogy Bars alone," Willa Bean replied. "That's another rule."

"You don't have to do it alone." Mama lifted Baby Louie out of his high chair. "I'll help you."

"You will?" Willa Bean sat up a little bit.

"Absolutely," Mama said. "I have to do some laundry first and then run over to Cloud Seven. We're out of fresh vegetables, and the milk is almost gone. Oh, and Baby Louie has a doctor's appointment at ten o'clock to make sure his wings are growing properly. So we'll have to get that out of the way, too, before we put him down for a nap. But after he falls asleep, I'm all yours, sweetheart."

Willa Bean's mouth dropped open.

Mama just didn't get it. Not even a little bit. She wanted to do something *now*. Not later, after a million-bajillion other things!

Just then, Ariel came into the room. Ariel was Willa Bean's older sister. She had long blond hair and liked to boss Willa Bean around. This morning, she had two beautiful rings on the tips of her white wings. One ring was green. The other was pink. Willa Bean frowned. She wasn't allowed to wear things like wing-rings yet. She had to wait one more year. Just because Mama said.

"How nice you look!" Mama said, giving Ariel a kiss on the cheek. "Your wing-rings are so pretty!"

"Thanks, Mama." Ariel tossed her long hair over one shoulder. "Some of my friends are going over to the Cubicles in a little while. Is it okay if I meet them there?"

"Of course," Mama said. "As long as you're home for dinner."

Willa Bean sat up straight in her chair. She wiggled her feet and bounced up and down. She loved the Cubicles. They were a group of shops on Cloud Six. She'd been there only once, with Mama and Baby Louie, but she thought it was a fun place to walk around. There were so many things to look at! And so much treasure to find!

"Oh!" Willa Bean said. "Can I go, too?"

Ariel glared at her little sister. "Not in a million years. This is *my* day with *my* friends."

"Please, Mama, let me go!" Willa Bean tugged on Mama's sleeve. "You know I don't have anyone to do things with today! Please make Ariel take me!"

"No way, sunray." Ariel looked at Mama. "I'm not going at all if I have to drag that little squirt around."

"Willa Bean." Mama knelt down in front of her. "I know this feels like a tough day. There's no school, and your plans with Harper can't happen. But Ariel wants to spend the day with her friends. So you're just going to have to think of something to do, honey. By yourself. And then in a little while, I'll be able to make a batch of Snoogy Bars with you. All right?"

It was not all right.

Not even a little bit.

In fact, it was horribly, terribly unfair.

Willa Bean could feel her inside crying feeling starting to rise in her chest.

But before it could come out of her mouth, she heard someone whispering her name. The whisper was coming from behind her, in the hallway.

"Willa Bean!"

She turned around.

Daddy raised his eyebrows and gave her a wave. "Come here, little love," he whispered. "I have an idea!"

Chapter 2

Super-Surprise!

Willa Bean squeezed in close to Daddy. She loved Daddy's ideas. They were always fun—and very exciting. "What is it?" she asked.

"How would you like to come to work with me today?" Daddy asked.

Willa Bean gasped. Daddy flew down to Earth every day to help big humans fall in love. It was very special cupid work. And very, very important. "You mean to Earth?" she whispered.

"The one and only," Daddy said.

"No teasing?" she whispered.

"No teasing." Daddy bent over and tugged one of her curls. "I could use some help, and it sounds like you've got time on your hands. What do you say?"

Willa Bean didn't say anything. Instead, she screamed and jumped up and down five times. Then she flew straight up into the air and bumped her head on the ceiling.

"Careful!" Daddy called.

"I'm okay!" Willa Bean was already flying back into the kitchen. "I'm going to work with Daddy!" she hollered overhead. "Daddy's taking me down to Earth so I can go to work with him! For real! No teasing!"

"Deasing!" shouted Baby Louie.

"Oh, honey." Mama's eyes were shiny. "How wonderful!"

"It's more than wonderful!" Willa Bean shouted. She swooped around the kitchen two times. "It's super-wonderful-times-a-million-bajillion!"

"Well, I'll take that as a yes," Daddy laughed, coming into the kitchen.

"You'll have fun, Willa Bean," said Ariel. "I remember my first trip down to Earth with Daddy. It was awesome." She frowned. "At least until we ran into that tiger."

Willa Bean fluttered back down to the floor. "Tiger?" she repeated softly.

"Ariel," Daddy warned, "there's no need to get into that story just now."

"Okay." Ariel shrugged. "Sorry. It was nothing, Willa Bean."

Willa Bean looked at her father. "Did you really run into a tiger?" Her voice quivered.

"Yes, we did," Daddy answered. "But my assignment was in India, where tigers are common. Besides, nothing happened. He barely even noticed us. We snuck right past, and that was the end of it. You and I are going to a place called England today. They don't have any tigers in England."

"But they might have bears!" Ariel called as she ran down the hall. "So be careful!"

"Bears?" Willa Bean's eyes were very round.

Daddy put an arm around her. "Ariel's just trying to scare you," he said. "The Cupid Rule must have slipped her mind entirely this morning. Don't pay any attention to her. We are not going to see any tigers or bears. I promise."

Willa Bean wondered if Ariel ever remembered the Cupid Rule, which went like this:

The very best way
To spend your day
Is to try to be kind—
All the time.

Willa Bean forgot it sometimes, too. But not as much as Ariel did.

"Double promise?" she asked Daddy.

"Double promise." Daddy held up two fingers and then pressed them against his lips. That was the double-promise sign.

"All right." Willa Bean wanted to believe Daddy. And she sort of did. At least most of her did. But there was a little part that stayed nervous. Miss Twizzle, her teacher at the Cupid Academy, had taught the class about Earth animals already. And tigers and bears did not sound like ones she wanted to bump into.

Not even a little bit.

"You have to get dressed, Willa Bean," Mama said. "You can't go to Earth in your pajamas!"

Willa Bean looked down at herself. She'd completely forgotten that she was still in her pajamas! She jumped up and down. "Can I wear my dressy dress with all the beaded feathers on the bottom?" she asked.

"I don't think that would be very practical," Mama said.

"There's no need to get fancy," Daddy said. "Just put on something comfortable. And hurry, Willa Bean. We have to leave in ten minutes, or I'm going to be late for my assignment."

Willa Bean raced for the steps.

"And brush that hair!" Mama called behind her. "No cupid of mine is going to Earth for the very first time with a head full of knots!"

Willa Bean ran into her room, yanked open the door to her closet, and pulled out her favorite play outfit. It was purple with silver polka dots. It matched her wings! "Snooze!" she yelled. "Snooze, guess what!"

"I can't imagine," Snooze said. He shook his head and rubbed his eyes with his wings. "But I doubt it's more exciting than the wonderful dream I was just having."

"Oh, it is!" Willa Bean wiggled her head through the top of her outfit and stuck an arm in each sleeve. "I'm going to work with Daddy! Down on Earth!"

"La Terre?" the little owl replied. Snooze used a lot of French words since he was from France. *La Terre* was French for *Earth*. "Are you sure?"

"Of course I'm sure!" Willa Bean giggled. "Daddy just said so!"

"When are you going?" Snooze cocked his head to one side.

"Right now!" Willa Bean yanked her brush through her mess of curls. It was not an easy thing to do. In fact, the brush got tangled in her hair. "Ooof!" she said as she tugged the brush. "It's stuck, Snooze!"

"Let me help you." Snooze flew close to Willa Bean's head. He gripped the hairbrush in his tiny talons. "Deep breath, *ma chérie*," he said. "This might pull a bit."

Willa Bean took a big breath. Snooze flapped his wings hard. He wiggled to the right, and then to the left, until the brush moved. Willa Bean scrunched up her face and bit her lip. Getting her hair untangled always hurt. "Almost there!" Snooze said. "Hold on!"

"Snooze?" Willa Bean gasped.

"Yes?"

"You've been to England before, haven't you?"

"Many times." Snooze made a little grunting sound and pulled again.

"Have you ever seen a tiger there?"

"Never," said Snooze.

"How about a bear?"

"A bear?" Snooze squealed. He pulled a final time on the brush, giving it a hard yank. Owl and brush went flying across the room.

"Snooze!" Willa Bean ran over and picked him up. "Are you all right?"

Snooze rubbed the back of his head. "I think so. But why in the world are you thinking about tigers and bears before your first trip to Earth?"

"Because Ariel said—"

Snooze held up a wing before Willa Bean could finish. "Ariel will say anything just to try to scare you. It's not very nice of her. More importantly, it's not accurate."

"What's *accurate*?" Willa Bean asked.

"*Accurate* means *correct*," Snooze told her. "Ariel is incorrect about tigers and bears living in England. There may be one or two in a zoo. But you certainly will not run into any of them in town."

"Willa Bean!" It was Daddy, calling from downstairs. "We have to go! Right now!"

"It's time!" Willa Bean shouted.

"Well, put me down first, please," Snooze said. "I have a full day of sleeping ahead, which I'd very much like to get on with."

"Oh, but you have to come with me!" Willa Bean begged. "Please, Snooze! It's my first trip to Earth!"

"Willa Bean, I was out all night," Snooze answered. "I went to Thailand and back, as a matter of fact. I have to get my rest. Otherwise, my brain won't work very well."

"Oh please, Snooze. *Pleasepleaseplease-pleasepleaseplease?*"

"You know, Willa Bean," the little owl

said as he settled himself on her shoulder, "you make it incredibly difficult to say no to some things."

"And you," said Willa Bean, leaning over to give her favorite flying friend an eyelash kiss, "make it incredibly easy to love you. All the time."

Chapter 3

Big Ben

"Hello, Snooze!" Daddy said as he put on his dark blue flight goggles. The strap went all the way around his head. They made his eyes look very big. "I didn't know you were coming with us today. How wonderful!"

"*Merci*," said Snooze. *Merci* meant *thank you* in French. "I'm looking forward to seeing you at work, Mr. Skylight."

Daddy handed Willa Bean a pair of goggles. They were much smaller than his and were bright yellow. "Put these on," he said. "They're Ariel's old ones, but they should fit."

"Why do I have to wear these?" Willa Bean asked as she stretched the goggles over her head.

"We'll be flying very quickly," Daddy said. "And moving through several different atmospheres until we get to Earth. It's important for your eyes to be protected from all the different kinds of light." He shifted the bag with his bow and arrows along his shoulder and tightened the buckle in front.

"Ooooh!" Willa Bean said, watching him. "That reminds me! Can I bring my arrows, Daddy?"

"There's no need for your arrows this time," Daddy said. "This trip is just for fun, Willa Bean. So you can watch what I do.

And maybe even help out if I need it."

"Oh pleasepleasepleaseplease?" begged Willa Bean.

"Here we go again," Snooze said.

"Please, Daddy," Willa Bean pressed. "Just so I can pretend? It'll be so much fun!"

Daddy's forehead furrowed into two deep lines. He glanced out the window to see where the sun was in the sky. "Okay, Willa Bean," he said. "But you have exactly five seconds to go get your arrows. One . . . two . . ."

Willa Bean flew off like a shot. She grabbed her quiver off her bedpost and started to fly out of the room. But as she did, all her arrows fell out. She gave a little yelp and went to pick them up. She could hear Daddy's voice downstairs. "Four . . ." She was running out of time! Quickly, she

stuffed the closest one into her quiver and
left the rest. Then she flew down the steps.

"Five!" Daddy stopped counting. "All
set?" he asked.

"All set!" Willa Bean said.

Snooze flew over and settled on her shoulder. "Where are the rest of your arrows, *ma chérie*? There's only one in here."

"I dropped them," Willa Bean said. "'Cause I was moving so fast. But it's okay. I can still pretend with one. And look!" She pulled out the pink arrow. "It's my Confidence arrow! So I can pretend a lot!"

"Indeed." Snooze nodded. "As long as you remember just to *pretend*. This is your father's trip, Willa Bean. He's working."

"Oh, I know." Willa Bean put the arrow back inside her quiver. "You don't have to worry about me, Snooze."

Mama and Baby Louie came outside to see them off. Mama waved as they jumped off Cloud Four and began to fly. "Goodbye!" she called. "Have a wonderful day! Listen to your father, Willa Bean! And have fun!"

"Good-bye, Mama!" Willa Bean waved behind her. "Good-bye, Baby Louie!"

Baby Louie was chewing on his red rubber star-bubble ball. He looked up when he heard his name called. "Dewey!" he said. "Dewey!"

Willa Bean turned back around. She could see everything through her yellow goggles. Daddy was on her right, and Snooze was on her left. What an adventure this was going to be! Her moody Moonday had completely turned itself around. Now it was a *mighty* Moonday!

♥

But it was a long trip. Much, much longer than Willa Bean thought it would be. She had never in her life flown so hard—or so far.

She had to get used to the clouds, too. Back in Nimbus, Willa Bean flew *around* their nine special clouds. Down here, a few miles from Earth, there were so many clouds that she had to fly *through* them!

It was fun flying through the clouds, especially since each one had a different smell inside. The first cloud smelled like dill pickles. Another one smelled like fresh orange peels. Willa Bean's favorite was one that smelled like butterscotch and hot chocolate. She wanted to turn somersaults inside that cloud, just to keep on smelling it. But Daddy kept going. And so she had to keep going, too.

Suddenly, Daddy yelled from up ahead. "Look down, Willa Bean! Look down!"

Willa Bean looked down. And for a moment, as she stared at the beautiful green-and-blue planet beneath her, she almost stopped breathing. It was too spectacular for words.

Emerald-green mountain peaks rose up through the sky. Great bodies of water glittered under the sun, and miles of sunbaked plains stretched out flat as a map.

"It's Earth!" Snooze shouted. "Isn't it marvelous, Willa Bean?"

Willa Bean nodded. She wanted to say yes. She wanted to say more than yes. She wanted to say yes a million-bajillion times. She wanted to say it was even prettier than in her dreams. But she was speechless. She couldn't say a single thing.

"We're headed down and to the right!" Daddy instructed. "Ten more minutes, and we'll be in London!"

"London?" Willa Bean finally found her voice.

"*Ah, oui,*" Snooze said, nodding. "London is the capital of England. It's a very large city. You're going to love it. Make sure to watch for Big Ben!"

"Big Ben?" Willa Bean felt a twinge of fear.

But Snooze had flown up ahead, closer to Daddy. He always flew faster when he got excited.

"Snooze?" Willa Bean called. "Who's Big Ben?"

Daddy and Snooze had already made their way into another enormous cloud. This one smelled like mint and lemons. Willa Bean flapped her purple wings with the silver tips harder, trying to catch up. Her breath was coming in little spurts, and her hands felt sweaty.

Who or what was Big Ben?

The name alone was scary enough.

BIG. BEN.

It sounded like a very BIG THING.

Worse than a tiger. Or a bear. Maybe it was a great big tiger-bear!

She flapped her wings very hard. "Snooze!" she called. "Daddy! Wait for me!"

In the next instant, she was out of the cloud. A few feet ahead of her, Daddy and Snooze hovered next to each other, waiting. Daddy had a big smile on his face.

"Look, little love!" he said. "Right over there! It's Big Ben!"

Chapter 4

Lovely London

Willa Bean raised her goggles and looked around quickly. There didn't seem to be any orange animals with black stripes. And she could not make out any furry brown things with big, sharp teeth. "Where?" she asked. "I don't see him!"

Daddy laughed. "That's because it's not a *him*. Big Ben is an *it*!" He pointed to a skinny building with a pointy top. Actually, there were two skinny buildings with pointy tops. But one of them had an enormous clock on the front. It was white with big black hands.

"Big Ben is a *clock*?" Willa Bean frowned.

"Well, Big Ben is a bell *inside* that clock tower," said Daddy. "It chimes so that the people of London can keep track of their day." He held a hand above his eyes and looked up at the sun. "And if I'm correct, it's about ten o'clock now. Which means you'll get to hear Big Ben for yourself soon."

"Wowww!" Willa Bean was so relieved that Big Ben was not a tiger or a bear that her "wow" came out in a whisper.

"You'll be impressed when you hear it," Snooze said. "It's the biggest chiming clock in the entire world. It makes a—"

A deep *BONG* cut off the rest of Snooze's sentence. It was so loud the air trembled around Willa Bean. It sounded again. And

then once more. Ten times the bonging noise shook the clouds. Willa Bean's feathers quivered and her hair boinged!

"Holy shamoley!" she shouted after it was all over. "Did you hear that?"

Daddy laughed. "Look, Willa Bean," he said. "Can you see that big river down there, just behind Big Ben?"

Willa Bean looked behind the big clock tower. A very long river wound its way through the city. It curved one way and then another.

"That's the Thames," Daddy explained. "It's a very famous river in England."

Willa Bean heard what Daddy said. But something across the river had caught her eye. Something round and enormous and so fun-looking that she almost flew on ahead all by herself, just to see what it was. Almost. "What's *that*?" she shouted, pointing.

"That," said Snooze, "is the London Eye."

"It's an *eye*?" Willa Bean drew back, horrified. "Like the ones in our head? That we see with?"

"No, no," Snooze said. "It's called an eye because it's round. It's a Ferris wheel."

"What's a Ferris wheel?" asked Willa Bean.

"It's a ride," Snooze replied. "Sort of like the ones back home at Waterworld. Except that there's no water. People sit in the seats, and it takes them up—way, way, way up—into the sky, and then it comes back down again."

Willa Bean wrinkled her nose. "What's the point of *that*?" she asked.

"Well, humans can't fly on their own," Daddy cut in. "But riding on something like the London Eye makes them feel like they're flying. At least for a little bit. It's exciting!"

"Earth people like to see what things look like from up here," Snooze added. "I think being up high makes them feel bigger."

Willa Bean already knew what most things looked like from here. They looked small. And far away. Sometimes they looked so small and far away that it was hard to make out anything at all. Why did humans want to look at things that were so hard to see? And how could looking at them make humans feel any bigger? It didn't make very much sense.

"We're heading down," Daddy said. "Stay close, Willa Bean. Watch out for telephone wires. And remember to keep your chin up when we land."

Willa Bean stayed between Daddy and Snooze as they flew toward the ground. She tried to remember all the things her flying teacher, Mr. Rightflight, had taught them at school about landing. *Head up. Arms in close. Eyes open at all times.*

They dropped lower, and lower still, until suddenly, with a skip and a bump, Willa Bean found herself standing on a sidewalk in London.

She had made it.

For the very first time in all her cupid years, she was standing on Earth!

Chapter 5

Angus's Anguish

Willa Bean looked around. Tall buildings stretched up on all sides of her. Some were so tall that from down here, they looked as if they were touching the sky. Which was funny, because when Willa Bean had been in the sky, she hadn't seen any buildings touching it.

There were strange little buggies, too, in all different colors, rolling up and down the streets. One buggy was not so little at all. It was bright red—and very, very tall.

In fact, it almost looked like the cloudbus she rode to the Cupid Academy every day!

"That's called a double-decker bus," Snooze told Willa Bean. "Double-deckers take people for rides all around the city."

"Oh, I want to go!" Willa Bean hopped up and down next to Daddy. "Pleaseplease-please*please*, Daddy, can we take a double-decker bus and ride around the city?"

"No, little love." Daddy flapped his wings. He flew high above the people on the sidewalk. "I must get to my assignment. Come on now. It's not much farther."

As she flew, Willa Bean watched all the Earth people rushing along the sidewalk below her. She did not have to worry about them seeing her. Cupids were invisible on Earth.

She swooped down low to get an extra-good look. There were girl people and boy people, too. Some of them were big, like Mama and Daddy. And some of them were small, like Baby Louie. There were in-between-sized people, too, like Ariel, and a few might have even been Willa Bean's size. But none of them had wings. Not even teeny-tiny, itty-bitty ones.

Willa Bean thought the girl people were lovely. A lot wore pretty scarves around their necks, and shoes that made clicking sounds against the sidewalk. Willa Bean loved that sound. *Click, click, click!* She wished she had shoes that made noises like that.

Just then, another noise caught her attention. "I don't want to go!" a little boy cried. He was hanging on to a woman's hand. Great big blubbering sounds came out of his mouth. "Please don't make me go, Mummy! The tiger will be there!"

Willa Bean stopped short. Her heart fluttered very fast. Had she heard him correctly? Had that little boy just said *tiger*?

"Oh, Angus!" the woman said. "Please don't make another fuss, dear. It will be all right, I promise. Now come on, or we're going to miss the second bell again!"

Angus did not seem to be worried about the second bell. He dug his heels into the pavement and tried to yank his hand loose from his mother's. He had curly orange hair and was dressed in a white shirt and brown pants. His shoes were brown, too, with red stripes along the sides.

"It won't be all right!" Angus wailed. "The tiger will be there! You don't understand anything!"

Willa Bean had heard enough. Quick as a shooting star, she caught up with Snooze.

"Snooze!" she whispered. "Did you hear what that boy just said?"

"No," Snooze said. "I'm trying to stay awake and keep up with your father, which is not an easy thing to do. Come on now, Willa Bean. He's already two whole streets ahead of us. We can't lose him."

"But, Snooze!" Willa Bean yanked on Snooze's tail a little.

"Ow!" said Snooze crossly. "That hurt!"

"I'm sorry," she said. "But that Earth boy just said something about a tiger! I heard him! With my very own ears!"

Snooze rubbed his tail feathers. He still looked cross. "Well, maybe his mother is taking him to the zoo. To see a tiger."

"But he's crying!" Willa Bean said. "He doesn't *want* to go!"

"Willa Bean." Snooze sighed. "Earth children cry about all sorts of different things. Try not to worry so much. Especially when you don't know the whole story."

Willa Bean looked down. By now, Angus's face was almost the same color as his hair. His mother was behind him, trying to push him across the street.

"Poor Angus," she whispered. "I don't like tigers, either."

"Come on, Willa Bean!" Snooze called.

"Hang on!" Willa Bean called to Angus. "It will be okay!"

She knew he couldn't hear her. Humans couldn't hear cupids at all. But it made her feel a tiny bit better just to say it. She flapped her wings slowly and looked over her shoulder as she flew away. Pretty soon, Angus was just a little orange dot in the background.

After a few more minutes, Daddy landed

next to a large brick building. Willa Bean and Snooze followed him. "Here we are," Daddy said.

In front of the brick building was a big sign. It had a picture of a tree on it. It read:

THE DAWLINGTON SCHOOL
8 DAWLINGTON STREET
MOGG BUTTONCAP, PRINCIPAL

Willa Bean looked at Snooze. Then she looked at the sign again. Finally, she looked at Daddy.

"Daddy," she said. "You must have the wrong place. This is a *school*. For Earth *children*. There won't be any grown-ups here for you to help."

Daddy grinned. "Who do you think teaches the Earth children?" He pointed to the last line of the sign. "My assignment

is to get Mr. Clive Peabody, a teacher here at the school, to ask Miss Mogg Buttoncap out on a date."

Willa Bean looked back at the sign. "*That* Miss Mogg Buttoncap?"

"Yes," Daddy answered. "Mr. Peabody is shy. He's had a crush on Miss Buttoncap for years, but he's never been able to work up the courage to tell her."

"Well, no wonder," Willa Bean said. "She's in charge! I wouldn't tell her, either!"

Daddy laughed. "Here's the best part," he said. "Miss Buttoncap has a crush on Mr. Peabody as well. And she's been hoping for him to ask her on a date for years!"

"Why doesn't she just ask *him*?" Willa Bean asked. "She's the principal! He has to say yes!"

Daddy laughed again. "It doesn't always work like that," he said. "Come with me. We'll go inside, and I'll show you how I do things."

Willa Bean felt a wiggling feeling inside her stomach.

She was about to see Daddy at work. His real work, where he would shoot one of his golden cupid arrows, so that an Earth person could fall in love.

Holy shamoley! Was there anything better than this in the whole entire universe?

It was going to be the most exciting day of her life!

Chapter 6

A Change of Plans

Daddy led them through the front doors of the Dawlington School. Inside was a long, empty hallway. The floor was white and shiny. Big pictures were taped to the walls—flowers and yellow suns and Earth people holding umbrellas under fat drops of rain. Willa Bean looked at all of them, but paused at the end. Her heart beat fast when she saw the last picture on the wall. "Snooze," she said softly, "come look at this one."

Snooze swung around to look at the picture. It had grass, and trees, and a large mountain in the middle. Gray clouds filled the sky. A fork of lightning poked out of the bottom of one cloud.

"Hmmm," said Snooze. "It's a bit different from the others, don't you think?"

"Look at the top of the mountain," said Willa Bean.

Snooze moved in close. "What is it?" he asked finally. "I can't quite make it out."

"It's a tiger." Willa Bean shivered. "See the black stripes? And the sharp teeth?"

"Ah," Snooze said. "Yes, now I see it. It's a very small tiger, isn't it?"

Willa Bean shuddered again. Small tigers or big tigers were still tigers. Both of them had sharp teeth and pointy claws and could run fast. Maybe, just maybe there was a tiger in this school. She took

a deep breath and closed her eyes. It was almost too scary to think about.

"Let's go, you two!" Daddy called. "Mr. Peabody's room is right up here! And, Snooze, remember to stay out of sight. We don't want anyone chasing after a loose owl in their school."

Willa Bean scooted close to Daddy, who had flown into a large room. Snooze flew behind the door. He stayed by the wall and did not make a sound. Snooze was not invisible like Daddy and Willa Bean were. Earth people could see him. And if an Earth person saw him—especially inside an Earth school—that could mean trouble.

There were lots and lots of children inside the room. But instead of sitting at their desks and doing work, they were all standing and moving around. A few of them were putting on sweaters and buttoning them up. One very big Earth boy put on a hat. It was red with a black band around the middle.

"Very good, children!" said a man at the front of the room. He was tall and thin, and he had a strange little patch of hair above his lip. "The faster you get in line, the faster we can go outside for recess!"

"Oh no," Daddy said. "It looks like we got here two minutes too late. Mr. Peabody is going to the playground with all the children. I'll have to wait until recess is over."

"That sounds just about perfect," Snooze said, yawning. "Now I'll get to take a nap."

"But, Daddy," Willa Bean said, "don't you have to wait until Mr. Peabody and Miss Buttoncap are in the same room?"

"That would be the easiest way," Daddy said. "But I might have to wait all day for that to happen. Sometimes I just help one person at a time."

Willa Bean frowned. She wanted to see Daddy in action. Right now. Why did they have to wait? "Why don't you just go outside?" she asked. "You could use one of your arrows on Mr. Peabody out there, couldn't you?"

"I'd rather not," Daddy answered. "My experience with Earth teachers during recess is that they move around a lot. My aim is better when they're standing still."

Willa Bean crossed her arms. "Hmph," she said.

Daddy put a golden arrow back inside his quiver. "I think I'll check on Miss Buttoncap," he said. "Do you want to come with me, Willa Bean?"

But Willa Bean didn't answer. She was

distracted. The children had begun to file out of the room. Mr. Peabody nodded as they passed, counting, "One, two, three . . ." Suddenly, Willa Bean's heart began to pound. There, almost at the end of the line, was a boy with curly orange hair.

"Willa Bean?" Daddy asked again. "Do you want to come with me?"

Willa Bean kept her eyes on Angus. She

could still see the dried tear tracks on his cheeks, and he shuffled his feet when he walked. He did not look like he wanted to go outside for recess.

Not even a little bit.

"Nimbus to Willa Bean Skylight!" said Daddy one last time.

Willa Bean turned around. "I think . . ." She hesitated. "I think I'll stay here with Snooze."

"All right." Daddy tugged gently on one of her curls. "It might be a good idea if you try to rest, too. It will be a long flight home."

"Bye, Daddy," Willa Bean said.

"See you in a little bit," Daddy answered.

"*Bonne nuit*, Willa Bean," said Snooze. *Bonne nuit* meant *good night* in French. Snooze curled up into a little ball behind the door. Then he draped a wing over his head and closed his eyes.

Willa Bean waited.

She counted to ten. Then she counted to twenty.

And finally, when she heard little snores coming from behind Snooze's wing, she flew out of Mr. Peabody's room and to the playground.

It was time to poke around—Willa Bean–style!

Chapter 7

The Tiger

The playground at the Dawlington School was full of wonderful things. There were swings and a seesaw and a big pole with a ball on a string. The children ran from one thing to the next, screaming happily. Mr. Peabody walked up and down the sidelines, talking to another teacher.

On the other side of the playground was an enormous square made up of red and blue and yellow metal bars. Some of the children were climbing the bars. Others were holding on to them and swinging from side to side.

Willa Bean had never seen such a thing before. She couldn't imagine what it was. But she didn't have time to wonder about it for long. She wanted to check on Angus. She wanted to make sure he was okay. And that he wasn't going to run into any tigers.

She flew straight up into the air, so that she could look down on everyone. It was much easier to see this way. She spotted Angus's curly orange hair right away.

But what she saw next made her heart beat fast again. The big Earth boy with the red hat was pulling Angus toward the metal thing with bars.

"I don't want to play!" Angus begged. "I told you, I don't like this game!"

"You do as I say!" the big boy snarled. "Or you'll make the tiger angry."

Willa Bean looked around frantically. Her heart beat even harder. Where was the tiger? Where *was* it? And what was this horrible boy going to do to Angus?

She watched as the big boy shoved Angus inside the metal thing with bars. At the sight of the big boy, the other children ran away. "You stay there." The big boy pointed a fat finger in Angus's face. "And don't you move."

Willa Bean gritted her teeth. Why was this boy being so mean? Hadn't he heard of the Cupid Rule? Didn't he know that the very best way to spend his day was to try to be kind—all the time?

She watched as the big boy climbed up the metal thing with bars. He moved very fast until he was at the top. Then he stood up and raised his arms to the sky. "I am the Tiger King!" he roared. "The biggest

and strongest in the whole entire world!
All the little babies must do as I say!"

Below him, Angus whimpered and
hung on to the bars.

Willa Bean fluttered nervously over-head, still watching.

The big boy scampered back down. He moved inside the bars until he was standing in front of Angus. Then he stuck out a finger again and poked Angus in the chest. "Say I'm the Tiger King!" he ordered.

"You're . . . the . . . Tiger . . . King." Angus struggled to get the words out. He was crying.

"Now say 'I'm a baby!'" The big boy poked Angus again. "Say it!"

Angus opened his mouth, but nothing came out. He was crying too hard.

"Say it!" yelled the big boy.

But Angus just covered his face with his hands and cried harder.

Suddenly, the big boy shoved Angus to the ground.

Willa Bean gasped.

Angus yelped as he fell. He held his knee against his chest. It was bleeding.

Just then, Mr. Peabody noticed the boys. He frowned when he saw Angus on the ground and hurried over. "Angus?" He looked at the big boy next. "Scully? What happened here?"

Scully took a step back. "Nothing," he answered. "Angus just fell."

"Angus?" Mr. Peabody said again. "Did you fall, or did Scully hurt you?"

Angus glanced nervously at Scully. He had so many tears rolling down his face that Willa Bean wondered if he could see anything at all. "I fell," he whispered.

NO! Nope, nope-ity, nope, nope, *nope*! Willa Bean flapped her wings furiously. This was not fair. This was not fair at all!

"Well, come with me." Mr. Peabody took Angus's hand and pulled him to his feet. "We'll take you to the nurse and get a bandage for that scrape."

Willa Bean watched Angus limp off the playground with Mr. Peabody. Then she turned around and glared at Scully. She had never been so angry in her whole entire life. What Scully had just done was so mean. And so awful. Plus, he'd gotten away with it. Just because Angus was scared of him.

Well, *she* was not going to let Scully get away with it.

Willa Bean watched Scully carefully for the rest of recess.

And by the time the bell had rung and the children had lined up to go back inside, she knew exactly what to do.

Chapter 8

Tigers Stink!

"Snooze!" Willa Bean shook her little owl awake as she flew back into Mr. Peabody's classroom. "Get up! Get up!"

Snooze woke with a start. He blinked a few times and stretched his wings. "Is it morning already?" He yawned.

"No, it's not morning." Willa Bean giggled. "It's almost the afternoon. And we're still at the Dawlington School on Earth."

"Ah!" Snooze ruffled his feathers. "Of course. Now I remember."

"You'll never guess what happened," Willa Bean said.

Snooze took a step backward. "Willa Bean," he said, "it makes me nervous when you say things like that."

Willa Bean leaned in close. "I found the tiger!" she whispered.

"The tiger?" Snooze looked around quickly. "What tiger?"

"The tiger in the picture!" said Willa Bean. "The tiger Angus was talking about!"

"Who's Angus?" Snooze tilted his head.

Willa Bean put a hand on her hip. "Snooze," she said, "haven't you been paying attention to anything?"

Snooze blinked. "Well, of course I have," he answered. "But that doesn't mean I've been paying attention to the same things *you've* been paying attention to."

"Do you want to see him?" Willa Bean whispered.

"See who?" asked Snooze.

"The tiger!" Willa Bean was impatient. "Who do you think I've been talking about?"

Snooze flapped his wings nervously. "It's in here? In the classroom?"

Willa Bean nodded. "Right behind this door."

Snooze took another step backward. His eyes were very round.

"Go ahead and peek," Willa Bean said. "The tiger is sitting in the third row, all the way in the back."

Snooze poked his head slowly around the door. He stared out at the children, who were sitting in their seats. Then he poked his head back out again. "There's a very large *boy* sitting in the third row all the way in the back," he said crossly. "You're playing tricks on me, Willa Bean."

"No, I'm not." Willa Bean peeked out from behind the door, too. She could go farther than Snooze because no one could see her. "That very large boy is named Scully. Also known as the Tiger King."

"The Tiger King?" repeated Snooze.

"Yes," Willa Bean said. "That's what he calls himself."

"So *he's* the tiger?" Snooze said.

Willa Bean nodded. "He's the meanest,

most horrible tiger-boy I've ever seen."

"That's not a very nice thing to say," Snooze said.

"I know," Willa Bean answered. "But it's true. He was awful to poor Angus out on the playground. He pushed him inside a big thing with bars, and he yelled at him. He told Angus to call him the Tiger King. And then he told Angus to call himself a baby. And when Angus wouldn't, he pushed him to the ground!"

"*Ah, non!*" Snooze exclaimed. "How terrible!"

Willa Bean nodded. "That's why Angus isn't even here right now. He's at the nurse, getting a bandage for his knee."

Snooze made a soft clucking noise inside his beak. "Very sad," he said. "Very sad, indeed."

"I know," said Willa Bean. She leaned in

and whispered, "That's why I have a plan."

"A plan?" Snooze repeated. "Willa Bean, you're not allowed to have any kind of plan. Remember?"

Willa Bean rummaged through her hair. There in the back, where the curls were the curliest, was her favorite blue pencil and her writing tablet. "Nifty Notes are the first part of the plan," she said.

Nifty Notes were mini-messages that cupids could leave for sad kids to make them feel better. They were only one or two words long. But they had to be mean-ingful. Sometimes it was hard to pick just the right words.

Snooze looked over her shoulder as Willa Bean began to write.

HANG ON!
TIGERS STINK!

"*Two* Nifty Notes?" Snooze asked.

"Yes," Willa Bean answered. "Angus definitely needs two."

She flew into the classroom and slipped the Nifty Notes inside Angus's desk. He would find them later when he came back from the nurse. She hoped they would

surprise him. And she hoped they would make him feel better.

Then she flew back to Snooze.

"That was very nice of you," Snooze said.

"Now we have to do one more thing—" Willa Bean started.

But before she could finish, Mr. Peabody walked into the classroom. Daddy flew in behind him.

"Hi, Daddy!" Willa Bean whispered.

Snooze tugged on Willa Bean's sleeve. "You were saying, Willa Bean?"

But Daddy put a finger to his lips. "Shh," he whispered. "The teacher is talking."

"Children, I will be out of the room for the next few minutes," said Mr. Peabody. "I would like everyone to copy the spelling words off the board. Scully Masterson, come with me, please."

Scully stood up. He fiddled with his belt buckle and bit his lip. Then he followed Mr. Peabody out of the room.

"Let's go!" Daddy said to Snooze and Willa Bean. "Mr. Peabody is taking the boy to see Miss Buttoncap! It's perfect timing! The adults will be in the same room, which means I can use my arrows on both of them at the same time!"

But Willa Bean frowned.

She needed to see Angus *before* Daddy used his arrows on Mr. Peabody and Miss Buttoncap. Not after. After, they would go back to Nimbus. And she'd never get to help Angus!

This was not how things were supposed to go.

Daddy was ruining everything.

And so was Mr. Peabody.

Chapter 9

LOVE!

Mr. Peabody led Scully Masterson down the wide, empty hallway. Daddy and Willa Bean followed them. Snooze, who was hidden inside Willa Bean's pocket, came, too.

Scully's brown shoes made a peeling sound against the floor as he walked. Mr. Peabody's shoes made a faint scuffing noise. Willa Bean marveled at all the different sounds shoes made on Earth. Clicking, peeling, scuffing. In Nimbus, where everyone walked on clouds, shoes made no sounds at all.

Finally, they stopped in front of a large green door. A sign on it said:

MISS MOGG BUTTONCAP

PRINCIPAL

PLEASE KNOCK!

Mr. Peabody pulled a handkerchief from his pocket. He wiped his upper lip with it and put it back. With a deep breath, he squared his shoulders and knocked on the door.

"Come in!" a woman's voice said.

"Here we go, Scully." Mr. Peabody opened the door. He let Scully walk in first.

Willa Bean stayed close to Daddy, who flew in quickly and settled himself in a

corner. Miss Buttoncap's office was not very big. It had a wide desk in the middle and two chairs in front of it. Miss Buttoncap was sitting behind the desk. Angus sat in one of the chairs. He was staring at the floor. A long rip stretched across the knee of his pants.

"Hello, Mr. Peabody." Miss Buttoncap stood up. Her cheeks turned pink. She had very blue eyes, and they were shining.

"Miss Buttoncap." Mr. Peabody nodded. He coughed and looked at his shoes.

For a few seconds, Willa Bean forgot all about her plan. It was so exciting to be in the same room with two Earth people who were about to fall in love! Any minute now, Daddy would help them seal the deal.

Miss Buttoncap cleared her throat. "Scully," she said in a firm voice, "have a seat, please."

Scully sat next to Angus.

Angus moved over just a little bit.

In the corner, Daddy began to fit one of his golden arrows into his bow.

Willa Bean reached around until her fingers felt the arrow she had picked up from her bedroom floor. It was her Confidence arrow. She knew she wasn't allowed to use it. Not today, when it was Daddy's assignment. Maybe not ever. Or at least not until she came down to Earth on a real assignment of her own with her class.

But there was someone in this room who needed her Confidence arrow more than anyone she could think of. She just had to find a way to send it flying—without anyone else knowing. Especially Daddy.

Miss Buttoncap came out from behind her desk. She was wearing a light blue skirt and a white blouse with short sleeves. Her hair was short and very dark. Willa Bean thought she was pretty. Not as pretty as Miss Twizzle, but then most people weren't. Except maybe Mama.

"I've just had a talk with Angus." Miss Buttoncap walked around the boys as she spoke. Her hands were behind her back, and she was not smiling. "It seems this is the third time in a week he's had to go to the nurse. Do you have any idea why, Scully?"

Scully slouched down in his seat. He kicked the desk a little and fiddled with the side of his chair.

"No idea?" Miss Buttoncap said. "Well then, let me help you out. Angus has told me that you have been bullying him. That you force him into the jungle gym on the playground at recess and make him call you the Tiger King. And if he doesn't do what you say, you push him. Is that correct?"

Angus stared at the floor. He pressed his lips together.

Daddy raised his bow until it was level with his shoulder. Willa Bean hovered close by, hardly breathing. It was here! Finally! She was going to see what happened when Daddy used his arrows on real Earth people!

But here were Angus and Scully, too! She couldn't miss a thing with them! She whipped her head back and forth. First Daddy. Then Angus and Scully. Then Daddy. Then—

With a soft whizzing sound, the golden arrow went flying from Daddy's bow. It hit Miss Buttoncap right in the arm, below her short sleeve. The arrow was invisible, of course, and being hit with it felt like a

soft pinch. Miss Buttoncap looked down at
her arm and put a hand over the spot. For
a moment, she seemed confused.

Suddenly, the color came back into her
cheeks. She glanced over at Mr. Peabody
and smiled.

Then, shaking her head, she squatted down next to Scully's chair and covered his hand with hers. "I will not tolerate meanness in my school, Scully Masterson." Her voice was quiet. "If you cannot be nice to people, especially to lovely ones like Angus Walker, you will not be allowed to play with anyone. Is that understood?"

Scully nodded once. He slumped down even farther in his chair.

Next to Willa Bean, Daddy was fitting another arrow into his bow. He let it fly before she could blink, and it soared across the room in Mr. Peabody's direction. Like Miss Buttoncap, Mr. Peabody looked down at his arm and then touched it. A pink glow colored his cheeks.

"All right, then," Miss Buttoncap said. "That will be all, boys."

"How about an apology?" Mr. Peabody

said, looking at Miss Buttoncap. His cheeks were getting pinker.

"Yes." Miss Buttoncap stared straight at Mr. Peabody. "That's a very good idea, Mr. Peabody. Scully? I think you owe someone in this room an apology."

Scully mumbled something that no one in the room could hear.

"What was that?" asked Mr. Peabody.

"I *said,* I'm sorry." Scully glared.

"Then how about a handshake?" Miss Buttoncap was still looking at Mr. Peabody. "Would that be out of the question?"

"Oh, no." Mr. Peabody looked as if he were sweating. He stuck out his hand to give Miss Buttoncap's hand a shake. "I think that's a great idea."

Miss Buttoncap laughed. She had small, pearly teeth. "I meant between the two boys," she said. "But all right." She took

Mr. Peabody's hand and shook it gently.

Willa Bean wiggled all over. Daddy had done it! Miss Buttoncap and Mr. Peabody were in love! She could tell just by looking at them! His golden arrows had worked!

"Well," said Daddy proudly, "I think things are pretty much finished here. Which means that now we can head home."

Willa Bean stopped wiggling. She did not want to go home yet.

She *couldn't* go home yet.

She still had to make things right for Angus.

And if Daddy and Snooze would just get out of the way and look in the other direction, maybe she could.

Chapter 10

An Extra Arrow

But Daddy and Snooze did not get out of the way.

And they did not look in the other direction.

"All right, boys," Mr. Peabody said, "we don't want you to miss out on your spelling words. Let's get back to class." He followed them out of the room. Just before he shut the door, Mr. Peabody turned around and gave Miss Buttoncap a little wave. She smiled and waved back.

"They'll be on a date by this weekend," Daddy said. "You can count on it." He straightened the quiver on his back and tightened his belt. "You two ready?" he asked. "I can't wait to get home. Mama said she was making Saturn Squares for dinner tonight!"

Willa Bean wasn't listening. She was watching Mr. Peabody lead Angus and Scully down the long hallway. Angus walked with his head down. And then, when no one was looking, Scully reached out and pinched his arm. It was starting all over again! In another few seconds, they would be back inside the classroom. Mr. Peabody would shut the door. Which meant that Willa Bean would lose her chance to help Angus forever.

Quick as a shooting star, she raced after them.

"Willa Bean!" Daddy shouted.

"Chérie!" called Snooze. "What are you doing?"

Willa Bean flapped her wings harder. She was only a few feet behind the boys now. Her heart was beating so hard she could hear it. She grabbed the arrow from her quiver, and lined it up on the bow. She had never actually done this before. She had practiced at the Cupid Academy, but she hadn't done it for real. And never on Earth. What if she missed? What if it didn't work?

She drew the Confidence arrow back as far as she could.

"Willa Bean!" Daddy yelled. "I told you no!"

Willa Bean knew she would get into trouble. She knew she had no right to do this. This was not her assignment. But

Angus needed her. And she did not want
to leave until she helped him.

She squinted until she could see her
mark.

"Willa Bean!" Daddy shouted again.

She squeezed her eyes tight. And then
she let the arrow fly.

The arrow shot out from her bow. It

wobbled a little to the right. It wobbled a little to the left. And then it hit Scully in the back of the leg.

SCULLY?

Willa Bean stared openmouthed as the mean boy stopped walking and rubbed the spot on his leg where the arrow had hit him. Then he started walking again. He caught up with Angus and Mr. Peabody and followed them inside the classroom.

Nope, nope-ity, nope, nope, nope! This wasn't how it was supposed to go at all! Not even a little bit!

Daddy flew up next to Willa Bean. "Wilhelmina Bernadina Skylight." He was frowning.

"I had to do it!" Willa Bean burst out. "I just had to!"

"You didn't have to do anything except watch and listen," Daddy said. "Which is exactly what you did *not* do. I'm very disappointed in you."

Willa Bean looked at the floor. Her eyes filled with tears.

"Let's go," Daddy said. "And I don't want to see you do a single thing on the way home except fly in a straight line behind me."

Willa Bean did as she was told. She flew behind Daddy as he led them out of the Dawlington School. When they passed Mr. Peabody's door, she couldn't help but peek in through the window. She could see Angus in his seat. Scully was in his. Both of them were sitting quietly, writing in their notebooks.

With a lump in her throat, Willa Bean flew on. She tried hard to stay in a straight line as they made their way out of London.

She whispered good-bye to Big Ben, and

to the river Thames, and to the London Eye. Would she ever see them again? Would Daddy ever take her anywhere again?

Daddy flew higher and faster as they went up. But Willa Bean did not fly quite so fast. Snooze flew next to her, to keep her company.

They passed through a raspberry-scented cloud without saying anything.

"I know you're sad," Snooze said finally. "But your father is right, Willa Bean. You were not supposed to use that arrow. It was just supposed to be pretend."

"I know." Willa Bean tried not to cry. "But I just couldn't stand it. I had to at least try to give Angus some confidence after that terrible day of his." Her wings drooped. "And then I hit Scully instead. The mean one! I can't do anything right."

"Well, I don't know about that, *chérie*,"

said Snooze. "You definitely should have listened to your father. But maybe you didn't use your Confidence arrow on the wrong person."

"What do you mean?" asked Willa Bean.

"Think about it," said Snooze. "The

only reason kids like Scully pick on other kids is because they don't feel good about themselves. Being mean makes them feel strong."

Willa Bean thought about this. "Remember what you said before, Snooze? About how some Earth people like to go up high because it makes them feel bigger?"

"I do," said Snooze.

"Well," said Willa Bean, "do you think Scully climbed way up high on that thing in the playground and yelled about being a tiger 'cause it made him feel strong? And maybe even bigger?"

"I do, indeed," Snooze said. "And that Confidence arrow is going to help him feel better about himself. He won't have to do silly things like yell about being a tiger or push smaller kids around. You never know, maybe he'll even stop being a bully."

"Wow," Willa Bean whispered. "Maybe he will."

Snooze didn't say anything. Then he flew up ahead.

"Snooze?" Willa Bean asked. "Where are you going?"

"Un moment," Snooze called over his shoulder. "I want to talk to your father."

Willa Bean stayed a good distance behind Daddy and Snooze. She watched as her little owl went on and on in Daddy's ear. She looked away when Daddy glanced back at her. She wasn't sure what was happening, but it made her a little nervous.

After another moment, Daddy and Snooze turned around. They flew on either side of Willa Bean as they drifted through a tangerine-scented cloud. "Let's take a break for a minute, Willa Bean," Daddy said. "Come up on top of the cloud."

Willa Bean followed Daddy to the top of the cloud. She watched as he pulled a tiny silver telescope out of his pocket and opened it. He pointed it toward Earth and looked through one end of it.

"What are you doing, Daddy?" asked Willa Bean.

"See for yourself," Daddy said, handing her the telescope.

Willa Bean held the telescope up to her eye. She looked through the lens.

"A little to the right," said Daddy.

Willa Bean turned it to the right. And what she saw made her gasp with surprise. There, through the window in Mr. Peabody's classroom, were Scully and Angus. They were laughing! Scully was patting Angus on the back!

"They're okay!" Willa Bean said, looking at Snooze.

Her little owl gave her a wink.

"I'm still not happy that you did something you weren't supposed to," Daddy said. "But I'm awfully proud of why you did it."

"You are?" Willa Bean said.

"I am." Daddy nodded. "Extremely proud. You turned that whole situation on its head, Willa Bean. Even if you didn't mean to. And both of those Earth boys will be better for it."

Willa Bean was smiling so hard that she couldn't say anything.

"Just promise me something," Daddy said. "The next time you come to work with me, let me know before you come up with one of your plans!"

"Double promise." Willa Bean held two fingers up to her lips and blew Daddy a kiss.

"Now let's get back to Nimbus." Daddy put an arm around her. "We can tell Mama all about it."

"Ariel too," Willa Bean said. "Wait till she hears about *my* tiger!"

Daddy and Snooze laughed.

And with a flap of their wings and a turn of their heads, they made their way back home.